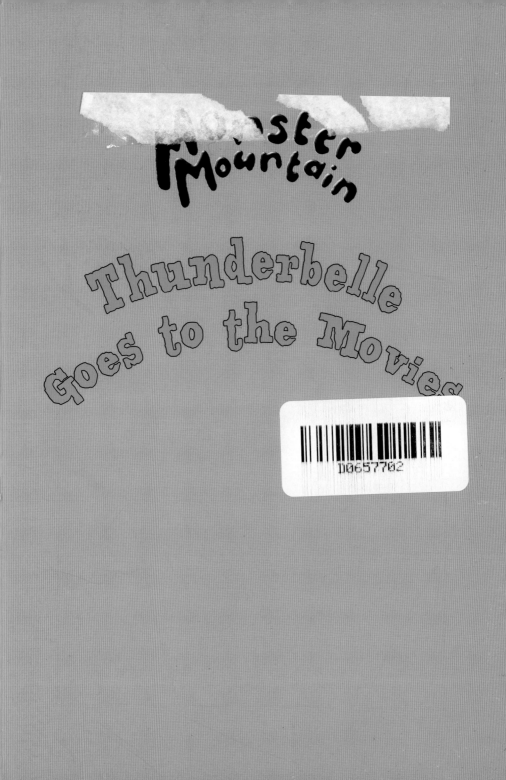

Monster
Mountain

Thunderbelle
Goes to the Movies

For Joseph Carolan
K.W.
For Joshua and Rachel,
with love
G. P-R.

First published in 2007 by Orchard Books
First paperback publication in 2008

ORCHARD BOOKS
338 Euston Road, London NW1 3BH
Orchard Books Australia
Level 17/207 Kent St, Sydney, NSW 2000

ISBN 978 1 84362 624 4 (hardback)
ISBN 978 1 84362 632 9 (paperback)

1 3 5 7 9 10 8 6 4 2 (hardback)
1 3 5 7 9 10 8 6 4 2 (paperback)

Printed in China

Orchard Books is a division of Hachette Children's Books,
an Hachette Livre UK company.

www.orchardbooks.co.uk

Monster Mountain

Thunderbelle Goes to the Movies

Karen Wallace

Illustrated by
Guy Parker-Rees

ORCHARD BOOKS

One morning Thunderbelle made
a decision.
"I'm going to be a movie star!"
she shouted.

Roxorus zoomed past on his
skateboard.

"Can I tell the other monsters?"
he asked.

"Of course," Thunderbelle said.

"Movie stars like lots of attention."

Thunderbelle had a book called
"How to be a Movie Star".
She read the first page. "Movie
stars wear pretty clothes."

Thunderbelle put on her prettiest dress.
She read the next page. "Movie stars
must look gorgeous."

Thunderbelle put on false eyelashes and a blonde wig.

She rubbed on bright blue eyeshadow.

She smeared on shiny red lipstick.
"You look just like a movie star,"
she told herself.

Pop!

Flash!

Flas

There was a knock on the door.
The other monsters rushed in.
Clodbuster took lots of photos.
Flash! Pop! Flash! Pop!

Roxorus asked lots of questions.
"What is it like to be famous?"
"Have you always wanted to be
a movie star?"

Mudmighty handed Thunderbelle
a big bunch of flowers. Thunderbelle
fluttered her eyelashes.

"Where's Pipsquawk?" asked
Roxorus suddenly.
Everyone looked round the room.
Pipsquawk wasn't there!

They heard a loud noise.

Bong! Bong! Bong!

It was the Brilliant Ideas gong.

Pipsquawk must be ringing it!

Clodbuster and Mudmighty ran
down the mountain as fast
as they could.

Thunderbelle had a ride on
Roxorus's skateboard.

Pipsquawk was hanging upside
down on a branch.
"What's your brilliant idea?"
cried Thunderbelle.

"Thunderbelle's a movie star,
right?" squawked Pipsquawk.
"RIGHT!" cried the monsters.

Pipsquawk spun round and round.
"And what do movie stars DO?"
The monsters looked at each other.
No one was sure.

"They make MOVIES!" squawked
Pipsquawk. "We're going to make
a movie!"
Thunderbelle jumped up and down.
"Pipsquawk! You're a genius!"

Pipsquawk wrote a story about
Thunderbelle in the jungle.

Clodbuster built
a movie camera.

Roxorus painted the
cliff white like
a movie screen.

Mudmighty turned his garden into a jungle. He also made a scary alligator for Pipsquawk.

While everyone else was busy,
Thunderbelle learnt her lines.

It was time to make the movie.
"Camera! Action!" squawked
Pipsquawk.

Thunderbelle stood in the middle
of the jungle.

"Here I am in the jungle,"
she cried. "Whatever will
happen next?"

"Very good," squawked Pipsquawk.
"Do it again, and this time,
look scared."

25

Thunderbelle frowned. "How can I look scared when I'm not feeling scared?"

"Pretend!" squawked Pipsquawk. "That is what movie stars do!"

Thunderbelle tried again but
nothing changed.
Pipsquawk winked at Mudmighty.
Mudmighty hid the scary alligator
behind Thunderbelle.

"One more time!" squawked
Pipsquawk. "Action!"
"Here I am in the jungle," cried
Thunderbelle. "Whatever will
happen next?"

Suddenly a great big alligator slid over her feet!

"EEEEEEKKKK!" screamed Thunderbelle. She fainted into Roxorus's arms.

"Cut!" Pipsquawk cried. "That was fantastic!"

That night the monsters watched
their movie.
They sat in a row and ate lots
of popcorn.
Everyone agreed it was greatest
movie ever.

It was called "When Thunderbelle
Met an Alligator!"

Monster Mountain

All priced at £4.99. Monster Mountain books are available from
all good bookshops, or can be ordered direct from the publisher:
Orchard Books, PO BOX 29, Douglas IM99 1BQ. Credit card orders
please telephone 01624 836000 or fax 01624 837033 or visit our website:
www.orchardbooks.co.uk or e-mail: bookshop@enterprise.net for details.

To order please quote title, author and ISBN and your full name and address.
Cheques and postal orders should be made payable to 'Bookpost plc.'
Postage and packing is FREE within the UK
(overseas customers should add £2.00 per book).

Prices and availability are subject to change.